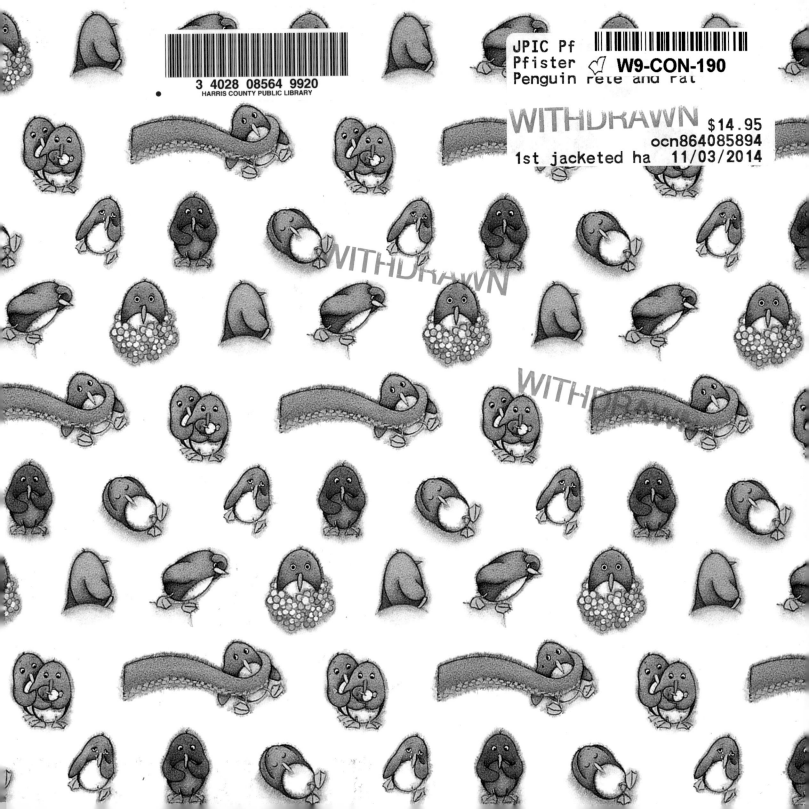

Copyright © 1989 by NordSüd Verlag AG, CH-8005 Zürich, Switzerland.
First published in Switzerland under the title *Pit und Pat*.
English translation copyright © 1989 by Anthea Bell

First published in the United States, Great Britain, Canada, Australia, and New Zealand in 1989
by NorthSouth Books Inc., an imprint of NordSüd Verlag AG, CH-8005 Zürich, Switzerland
First jacketed hardcover edition published in 2013.

Distributed in the United States by NorthSouth Books Inc., New York 10016.

Pfister, Marcus.
[Pit und Pat. English]
Penguin Pete and Pat / Marcus Pfister: translated by Anthea Bell.
Translation of: Pit und Pat.
Summary: Upon returning from his travels, Penguin Pete is captivated by a girl penguin with
a blue beak, cultivates her friendship, and wins her flipper in marriage.
ISBN: 1-55858-003-4
[1. Penguins—Fiction.] 1. Title.
PZ7.P448558P1 1989
[E]—dc19      88-25296

British Library Cataloguing in Publication Data
Pfister, Marcus, 1960—
Penguin Pete and Pat.
1. Title
833'914[J]

Printed in China by Leo Paper Products Ltd.,
Heshan, Guangdong, September 2013.

ISBN: 978-0-7358-4155-0

1  3  5  7  9  •  10  8  6  4  2
www.northsouth.com
Meet Marcus Pfister at www.marcuspfister.ch

Written and illustrated by
**Marcus Pfister**

*Translated by  Anthea Bell*

# PENGUIN PETE
# AND PAT

**North South**

**P**enguin Pete woke up slowly. For a moment he didn't know where he was.

"Good morning," a deep voice rumbled. "Did you sleep well?"

"Oh, it's you, Walter!" said Pete, slightly startled. "I thought I was still dreaming!"

Pete climbed Walter Whale's tail fin and looked out over the sea. He blinked drowsily in the first rays of the sun.

The two friends had been on their travels for three weeks now, and it would soon be time to go home.

"Before we swim back, I want you to meet my cousins the dolphins," said Walter. "Come on, let's dive down!"

Pete clung to the whale's tail fin, and down they went.

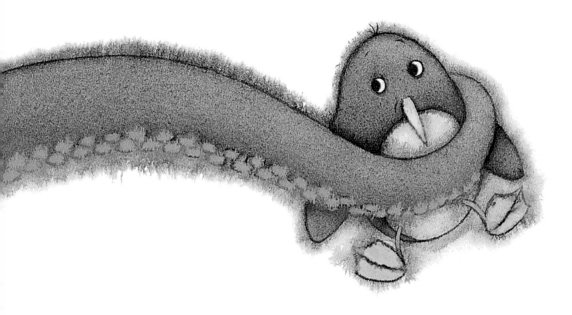

They hadn't been under the water for five minutes
when Pete felt a long arm snatch him away from the
whale. Then a second arm seized him, then a third, and
then more and more arms. Everything suddenly went dark.
   "Help!" shouted Pete, as loud as he could. "Walter, help!"
   "Calm down! No need to be worried while I'm around,"
said Walter's soothing voice. Pete was very glad to hear him.
"This is my friend the octopus. He's always fooling about."

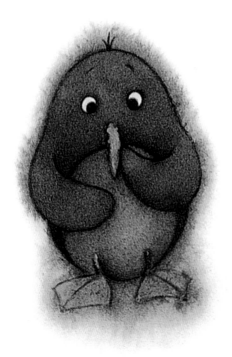

Pete's feathers were covered with octopus ink. He could hardly move his flippers. So the two friends came up to the surface and Pete showered under the whale's jet of water until he was nice and clean again.

"Look, there are the dolphins leaping about ahead of us!" cried Walter happily.

Pete and Walter swam so close to the dolphins that Pete could almost touch them. They leaped gracefully out of the water, right up in the air, and then fell back into the cold sea.

"When we get home I'll show my friends how the dolphins leap," said Pete. "Won't they be surprised!"

So Walter and Pete swam the shortest way back to the penguin colony.

The news of Pete's return spread like lightning. All the penguins came to welcome him. When Pete stepped ashore, a girl penguin went up to him and gave him a bunch of flowers. Pete couldn't take his eyes off her beautiful blue beak. But before he could say thank you, his friends carried him away on their shoulders in glee.

Pete's friends put him down when they reached the mound of snow where he lived. Father and Mother Penguin were glad Pete was back. They were surprised to see how big he had grown.

He told them about his adventures until late in the night. Then it was time to go to sleep. But Pete couldn't sleep for a long time. He kept thinking of the girl penguin.

"I'll go and look for her tomorrow," he murmured, as he finally closed his eyes.

Just before sunrise, Pete set off in search of the girl penguin with the blue beak. From the top of the highest hill, he could see the whole island. But there wasn't a sign of her anywhere.

Pete asked all the penguins he met, but none of them had seen her. He was just beginning to feel discouraged when someone finally said, "Oh, you mean Pat! She's in the little bay over there."

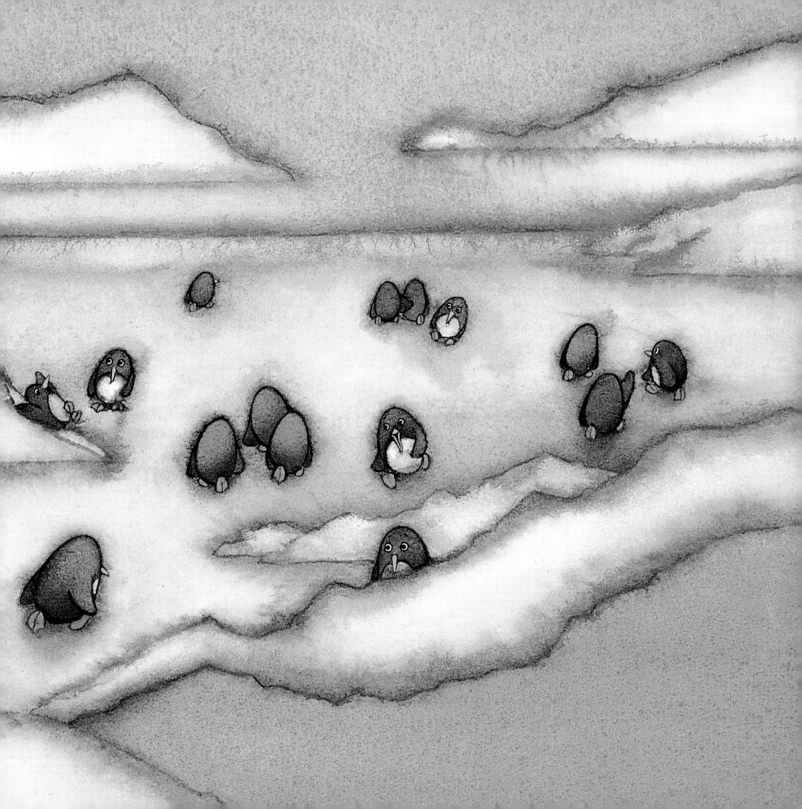

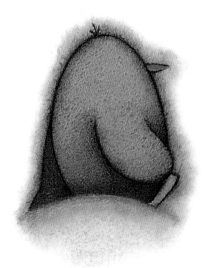

Sure enough, Pete found the girl penguin with the blue beak on the icy shores of the little bay. She was startled when Pete suddenly spoke to her.

"Hello, Pat!" he said. "I didn't have time to say thank you for the lovely bunch of flowers yesterday. Would you like some ice?"

Pat was very pleased when Pete broke off a big icicle and sat down beside her. They took turns licking the icicle as they told each other all about themselves.

They were soon close friends, and after that they met every day. And when at last Pete plucked up the courage to ask for Pat's flipper in marriage, preparations were made for a big wedding party on the island.

As a special surprise, Walter invited everyone Pete had met on his travels to the wedding: the little boy with his sleigh dog, the sea lions and dolphins, the elephant seal and the octopus, and even the little bird Steve. They danced all night on the smooth ice, and didn't go home till nearly morning.

Pete and Pat soon began building a nest, and Pat laid an egg. After nearly forty days their baby penguin Tim hatched out.

Pat took him carefully in her flippers, and Pete looked proudly at Tim's beak. His son was the only penguin for miles around to have a green beak!

Tim grew fast. He often played in the snow all day long, but one day he came home in tears.

"All the others say I'm green just because I can't swim!" he sobbed.

"Don't worry, Tim," Pete comforted him. "It's only your beak that's green! My friends laughed at me when I was little too. But I know something you'll enjoy—something that will really surprise the others! Come with me!"

And Tim was allowed into the water! Pete let him ride on his tummy. All the others were amazed, and none of them laughed at Tim anymore.

After that, Tim went riding through the water every day until he was big enough to swim by himself.

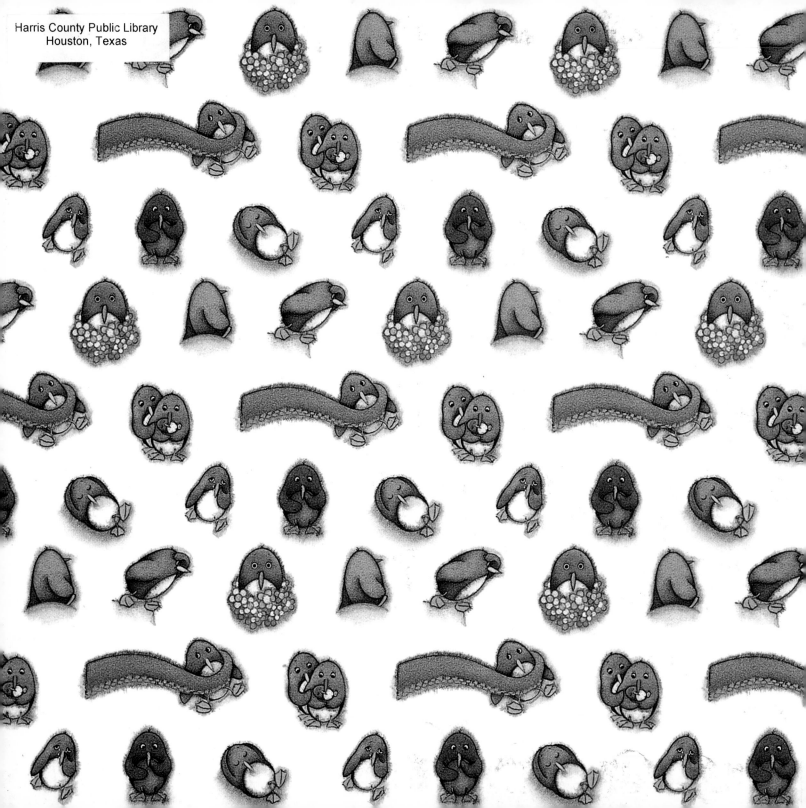